Two Piano Tuners

M. B. Goffstein

TWO PIANO TUNERS

Farrar, Straus and Giroux

New York

12759

E
G

*To my husband
and our memory of Walter Hupfer*

Two Piano Tuners

Every morning Reuben Weinstock, the piano tuner, got stiffly out of bed, and washed and shaved in hot water at the kitchen sink. Then he went into his bedroom and brushed his thick gray hair, got dressed in a clean shirt and trousers, put his beautiful old maroon wool robe over them, and tying the silky tasseled cord around his waist, went back into the kitchen to start breakfast cooking.

He put water on the stove in a blue and white enameled saucepan and an old yellow coffee pot. Then he opened the cupboard and set the table with a blue plate and an orange plate, a navy-blue bowl and a green bowl, plaster salt and pepper shakers that had seashells stuck into them and bright red plastic tops, two white paper napkins, two knives and two spoons with yellow plastic handles, and two big white cups.

Almost everything in the cupboard had been given to Reuben Weinstock two years ago by the ladies whose pianos he tuned, when they heard that his son and daughter-in-law had died in another town and left him their little girl.

"But how can you take her?" Mrs. Perlman had asked him kindly. "You are a widower, Mr. Weinstock, and you are not a young man any more, either. What can you give her?"

"Well, I know music," he had said. "I know music. I have tuned pianos for all the great pianists, and I used to travel with Isaac Lipman. I can teach the little girl to play the piano and she might become a great concert artist!''

"Or a piano teacher," agreed Mrs. Perlman.

Almost all the ladies had given him something— dishes, little dresses, a small bed and dresser. "And if you need any advice, please feel free to ask me," every one of them said.

By the time he finished setting the table, the water on the stove was boiling. Reuben Weinstock gently dropped three brown eggs into the blue and white saucepan, measured coffee into the yellow pot, took out a bottle of milk and a dish of butter, and put four slices of bread on the toast rack. Then he slowly went upstairs, holding on to the rail.

There was only one room upstairs, a big low-ceilinged room. When Reuben Weinstock climbed the top step, he was standing right in the middle of it, looking down at a long little bump under a fuzzy blue blanket.

"Debbie," he whispered. "It's morning, Debbie."

The long bump curled into a round ball under the blanket.

"Wake up, little Debbie!"

"Hm-m-m-m-m," sang the bump. "Hm-m-m-m-m."

"Hm-m-m-m-m," sang Mr. Weinstock, a little bit lower. "Hm-m-m-m-m. I'm afraid you are sharp again this morning, Debbie."

She jumped out of bed in her long pink pajamas and ran downstairs to play middle C on the piano: C! C! "You are right, Grandpa Reuben," she

6

called, and went into the kitchen to wash her face and brush her teeth at the sink.

When she came back upstairs, her bed was made and Mr. Weinstock, whose back ached from bending over, was laying out her clean clothes on it.

"Oh no, Grandpa!" cried Debbie. "Not my jumper! Don't you remember that I don't have school today, so I don't have to wear my jumper?"

"I thought you wanted to come with me to the Auditorium, to tune the grand piano."

"Of course I do!"

"Would you like to wear a prettier dress?"

"I want to wear pants."

"Not to go with me," said Mr. Weinstock.

"Oh, Grandpa Reuben," stormed Debbie. "I want to *help* you."

"Then put on your jumper," he said, stroking her bushy hair kindly, "and if you can play your piano lesson well this morning, you may carry my black bag into the Auditorium."

"Will the pianist be there?"

"I think so."

"And won't he be amazed to see a little girl coming to tune that piano?"

"He certainly will be," agreed Mr. Weinstock as he began to make his way carefully downstairs.

"If he thinks I tuned the piano, he won't show up for the concert," chuckled Debbie, who had dressed and gotten downstairs at his heels. "He'll be too scared!"

After breakfast, while Mr. Weinstock cleared the kitchen table, washed the dishes, and swept up the crumbs, Debbie played her piano lesson for him. It was *Reverie,* by Felix Mendelssohn, and she had been playing it for the past three weeks.

Now Mr. Weinstock came in, drying the last dish. "It is still not so good," he said sadly.

Debbie jumped down from the piano stool. "I know it," she said. "We have to tune this old piano again."

She started to raise the lid, but Mr. Weinstock went back into the kitchen to hang up his dish-towel, saying, "We must leave for the Auditorium. Get your coat and hat, Debbie—and brush your hair."

Then he went into his bedroom and changed

from his robe to the jacket that matched his dark blue pants. He tucked a clean handkerchief into his pocket and helped Debbie on with her coat.

"I'm sorry you played so badly," he said as he tied her hat strings under her chin.

But when they got to the Auditorium, he handed her his black bag anyway, and Debbie proudly carried it inside.

The pianist *was* already there, but he did not even see her. "Reuben!" he cried, and hurried up the aisle, past rows of empty seats, to hug Mr. Weinstock.

"Isaac!" Mr. Weinstock hugged him back.

They kept their hands on each other's shoulders and beamed at each other. "You look well! You look well!" they said.

"But what are you doing here?" asked Mr. Weinstock.

"You were expecting Walter Bernheimer?"

"Yes!"

"I heard from my manager that he couldn't get here, and I decided to surprise you. I have been on the train since yesterday morning, in order to play here this afternoon."

"You! Oh, that's wonderful. Oh, now we'll hear some real music!"

"And I, once again, after all these years, will play on a piano that is perfectly tuned," said the great concert pianist.

He looked down, as if to make sure that Reuben Weinstock had his bag of tuning instruments with him, and he saw Debbie, still holding on to it.

"Who is this?" he asked.

"This is the piano tuner," joked Mr. Weinstock. He put his hand on Debbie's shoulder. "This is my granddaughter, Deborah Weinstock, who came to live with me two years ago."

"And I really *could* tune that piano."

"You could?"

Debbie nodded uncertainly.

"I want her to play the piano and she always wants to tune or make repairs."

"That kind of work isn't good for a pianist's hands," Isaac Lipman warned her.

Debbie tucked her hand into her grandfather's hand. "Well, I'm going to be a piano tuner," she said.

"Your grandfather is the best piano tuner in

the world, you know, so I hope you are taking good care of him."

"I'm going to," said Debbie.

Isaac Lipman put his arm around Mr. Weinstock for a moment. "Now I must go back to the dressing room and rest," he said. "Please come back when you have finished your work and we'll have a good visit."

They all walked down the aisle together. Isaac Lipman went up onto the stage and disappeared, while Mr. Weinstock and Debbie took off their coats and hats and laid them on two chairs in the front row. Then they took off their overshoes and went up the stairs to the stage.

Mr. Lipman had been practicing before they came, so the grand piano was already open and the top was up. Mr. Weinstock slid out the music rack and carried it to the back of the stage and leaned it up against the wall.

Then he went back to the piano, sat down, adjusted the bench, and played a few notes. He got up again to take off his jacket and hang it over the back of a wooden chair that was standing near the piano, and he rolled up his shirt sleeves.

Debbie had set his bag down on the floor beside the piano bench. Mr. Weinstock knelt down and opened it and took out his tuning hammer and screwdriver, a strip of red felt, and two little gray felt wedges. He took his tuning fork out of its case and put the case back into his bag.

He stood up and laid the red felt strip inside the piano and began to poke it between the strings with his screwdriver. Then he fitted the tuning hammer onto a pin, hit the tuning fork against his knee and touched it to the metal frame, listened, sat down again, and began to tune the grand piano.

C! C! C! he played. C! C! C! And he pushed the hammer a little to the left. C AND C! F AND C! G AND C! G AND D! F AND D! A AND D! He played each interval over and over again, turning the tuning pins one at a time with the tuning hammer, winding the piano strings more tightly or loosening them a little, until each note was pure and beautiful.

F AND A! F AND A! Debbie stood looking into the piano, at the long line of strings, the heavy iron frame, the yellow wood sounding board, and the flat black dampers, and hummed the notes that were being tuned. She was enjoying the feeling she had of being able to sing two notes at a time.

She always knew which notes would come next; she knew the whole tuning pattern by heart. She thought it was beautiful and exciting, and she liked it better than any music she had ever heard.

"Please stop that, Debbie," said Mr. Weinstock. "I can't hear anything when you hum."

Debbie put her hand over her mouth and Mr. Weinstock went on tuning: A AND E! A AND E! G AND E! E AND B! Then Debbie forgot and started humming again.

"Debbie!"

"I'm sorry, Grandpa."

G AND B! B AND D! G AND B AND D! G
AND B AND D! B AND F-SHARP! F-SHARP
AND A! "Debbie?" said Mr. Weinstock.

She looked at him in amazement. "I wasn't
humming!"

"No, I just remembered that I'm supposed to
tune Mrs. Perlman's piano too, this morning."

"Oh," said Debbie.

"Would you go over to her house now, and ask
her if I may do it tomorrow instead?"

"Do I have to go now, before you're through
working on this piano?"

"I would like you to, so you'll be back in time
to visit with Mr. Lipman."

"But are you going to take out the action?"

Debbie loved to see the long row of hammers, with their thin shanks and workmanlike red and gray and white felt tops, flip up when Mr. Weinstock hit the keys. She liked the files, the grease, the needles, and all of the good little tools her grandfather might use if he took the action out of the piano.

"No," said Mr. Weinstock. "Mr. Lipman didn't say that there was anything wrong, and everything seems fine to me."

"But you might have to change a string."

"I hope not. Anyway, you've seen me do that a hundred times."

"I like it when they break," said Debbie.

"Well, you'll be back long before I'm done!"

So Debbie walked across the front of the stage,

down the steps, and over to the seat that held her coat and hat. She put them on, then sat down to buckle her overshoes.

"Can you do everything by yourself?" Mr. Weinstock called from the stage.

"Yuh," said Debbie, holding her hat strings down with her chin while she tried to make a bow.

But Mr. Weinstock came down to help her. "Now, you be sure to tell Mrs. Perlman that Isaac Lipman is here, so she won't miss the concert this afternoon. And ask her if it's all right to tune her piano tomorrow."

"I will."

"Be very careful."

Debbie nodded seriously. She walked up the dim, empty aisle alone, opened the door, and went into the lobby. She took a drink from the drinking fountain, then she pushed open one of the heavy front doors and went outside. It had been snowing just a little, not enough to stick.

She went down the wide, gray stone steps to the sidewalk. Two big dogs, one black and one tan, and a little spotted dog stood talking together on the corner. "Hello," thought Debbie. "Hello, dogs, here comes the piano tuner!"

She crossed the street and started up the long block, looking at each house as she passed it: the white one with red shutters, the dark green one with yellow trimming, the pretty little gray house with soft brown bushes in front and a baby looking out the window. "There goes the piano tuner," she thought for the baby.

And she went past Mrs. Perlman's brown house

28

with white lace curtains in the windows. She was going home first!

Their house was painted yellow, with a dark red roof. It was at the end of the block, behind a grassy, empty lot. Debbie cut through the lot and went in the back door and through the kitchen.

In the living room, next to the piano, was a bureau with a lot of old tuning instruments in its bottom drawer. Debbie sat down on the carpet and pulled the drawer out. She took out the tuning hammer that Reuben Weinstock never used because its handle was too long. It was a little bit rusty, but so was the only tuning fork Debbie could find that said C on it. She found one gray felt wedge and one black rubber one.

Debbie brought them upstairs to her room and

put them on the bed while she took off her coat, got out of her jumper, stepped into her pants, and put the coat back on. The pants had an elasticized waistband which was perfect for holding the tuning hammer up inside them, and she put the tuning fork and wedges into her back pocket. She buttoned her coat on the way downstairs and went out the door, back through the vacant lot, and down the block to Mrs. Perlman's house.

She climbed the front steps and pressed the doorbell, and waited for a long time. Finally she pressed the bell again.

"Why, Debbie," said Mrs. Perlman, opening the door. "I looked out the window before, but I couldn't see anyone!"

"That's all right," said Debbie.

"Won't you come in?"

"My grandpa says, he hopes you don't mind if I tune your piano."

"What?"

"Well, his friend Isaac Lipman came to give a concert, and he says you should come."

"Isaac Lipman came here?"

"He's at the Auditorium, and Grandpa Reuben is tuning the piano for *him* instead of for Walter Bernheimer," Debbie explained.

"Do you mean to say that Isaac Lipman is giving a concert here, this afternoon?"

"Yes, and I have to help my grandpa. He asked me to come and tune your piano."

"Oh, how thrilling!" exclaimed Mrs. Perlman.

"I'll do a good job," said Debbie, taking off her coat on her way over to Mrs. Perlman's little upright piano in the living room.

"But—" said Mrs. Perlman. "Oh, what does it matter?" she thought. "She's too little to hurt anything, and Mr. Weinstock will certainly do it over again, anyway." So she followed Debbie into the living room and began to take the little round lace doilies and candy dishes and china figurines away from the top of the piano.

Debbie put her coat and hat down on a slippery satin chair, and took off her overshoes and put them in the hall. Then, when Mrs. Perlman had finished clearing the piano top, she helped Debbie raise the lid and pull off the front panel. They set it carefully down on the carpet and leaned it against the wall.

Debbie pulled the tuning hammer out of her waistband, the tuning fork and wedges out of her pocket, and sat down at the piano, looking at the strings. There were two strings for each note.

She hit the tuning fork against her knee, held it to a part of the metal frame, listened to it carefully, and then tried the piano: C! C! C! C!

"Would you like to have some cookies and a glass of milk, Debbie?"

"Maybe later," Debbie said. She fitted her tuning hammer onto the pin that held the first string for middle C, and put a wedge between the other C string and the first C-sharp string.

She hit the tuning fork against her knee again, and held it to the metal frame, and listened very, very closely. C! C! she played, and pushed the hammer. C! C! C! C! C! The gray felt wedge fell out, and Debbie put it back. C! C! C! C! C! C! C!

She wished that Mrs. Perlman wouldn't keep standing right beside her.

Luckily, Mrs. Perlman, who had always been a great admirer of Isaac Lipman, felt that she could not wait another minute to decide what to wear to his concert. She patted Debbie on the shoulder and ran upstairs.

As Reuben Weinstock finished tuning the bass notes on the grand piano in the Auditorium, he thought to himself that Debbie should be back any moment. He moved his tuning hammer and screwdriver up to the top of the piano, pushed wedges between the strings, and started tuning the treble notes.

He kept looking at the door while he worked,

and by the time he had finished tuning the treble and testing the whole keyboard up and down, and Debbie still had not come, he felt very, very worried. He put his tools back into his black bag, shut it, and sat back down on the piano bench, with his eyes on the door.

"Reuben," said Isaac Lipman, coming onto the stage behind him, "if only I had known what a comfortable couch there is in the dressing room in this Auditorium, I would have come here before. I had a wonderful sleep!"

Mr. Weinstock turned to look at him but did not smile.

"What's the matter?" asked Isaac Lipman. "Where did that little granddaughter of yours go? I want to hear her play."

Mr. Weinstock stood up. "I sent her to ask one of our neighbors, who lives only a block away from here, if I may tune her piano tomorrow instead of today, because you are here. She should have been back an hour ago."

"She probably stayed there to tune it herself," said Mr. Lipman. "Let me try the piano while we are waiting for her. Then I want to take you both out to lunch."

He sat down and began to play. "Bravo!" he said. "Bravo, Reuben. There are few enough good piano tuners in the world, but there is only one Reuben Weinstock."

But Mr. Weinstock had left the stage and was standing in front of the first row of seats, putting on his coat and hat. "Thank you," he said. His hands were shaking and he could hardly button his overcoat.

"Are you going out to find the little girl? Just wait a minute and I'll come with you. I think a little walk would be good for me after that nap." And Isaac Lipman went backstage to get his things from the dressing room.

"She hasn't come back yet? All right, let's go," he said, coming down from the stage wearing his coat and scarf and a black fur hat.

"I'm so sorry this had to happen today, while you are here—and before your concert," Mr. Weinstock said to him as they walked up the aisle. They went through the lobby and outdoors.

"I'm only sorry because of you," said Isaac

Lipman. "You don't look well, Reuben. You seem very tired. I'm afraid it has been hard on you, taking care of that little girl."

"She is my son's child," said Mr. Weinstock. "He and his wife died two years ago."

"I'm sorry, Reuben."

"Now Debbie is all I've got," said Mr. Weinstock. "But she is so much!"

The two men walked up the block in silence, looking all around for Debbie, or for anyone who might have seen her. A big black dog trotted ahead of them for a while, then he turned off at the house with the baby.

A minute later they came to Mrs. Perlman's house and Reuben Weinstock stopped. "This is where she was supposed to come," he said.

A AND E! A AND E! A AND E! they heard

in the damp air. A AND E! A AND E! A AND E!

"Ah," said Isaac Lipman. "You see, I was right!"

"But how—" began Mr. Weinstock. "But she will ruin the piano!" he said. "She doesn't know how to tune a piano. She has never tuned one before."

"If she has been living with you for two years, then I'm sure she knows how. But Reuben, she is very naughty!"

Mr. Weinstock put his hand on his friend's arm. "Don't say that. Thank God, she is safe. Whatever she has done to the piano, I can fix. She probably meant to help me. She always wants to help me!"

"She *should* help you, Reuben."

"She is only a little girl. I don't want her to help

me; I have to help her. I am giving her piano lessons—that is all I can give her. But I have been hoping that she will be a concert artist someday."

"When I was her age, I had already played for the Empress of Russia," said Isaac Lipman. "Reuben, your little granddaughter may be as talented as I am. But if she doesn't want to be a pianist more than anything else in the world, she will certainly never be one. She says she wants to be a piano tuner, so let's see how well she is tuning that piano." And taking Mr. Weinstock's arm, he marched up the walk to the front door and pressed the bell.

They stood on the top step and listened to Debbie's tuning until Mrs. Perlman opened the door. "Oh!" she gasped.

"Mrs. Perlman, may I present Mr. Isaac Lipman?" said Mr. Weinstock.

"How do you do. I'm so thrilled to meet you! I recognized you from your picture. Do you know, I have your autograph? I've kept it for twenty years. Debbie said you were here. She's in the living room, tuning my piano. Come in, come in!"

They wiped their feet on the mat and took off their boots. Then they followed Mrs. Perlman into the living room, wearing their coats and holding their hats.

Debbie was standing between the piano bench and the keyboard, looking impatient and unhappy. "I've only done two octaves," she said.

"You shouldn't have done any," said her grandfather. "You should have come right back to the Auditorium. I was very worried about you."

"Won't you take off your coats and sit down?" Mrs. Perlman was asking.

"Mr. Lipman can't—" began Mr. Weinstock.

But Isaac Lipman took off his coat and scarf and handed them to Mrs. Perlman. "Thank you very much," he said. "I am sorry to trouble you."

"It's not any trouble. It's an honor!" said Mrs. Perlman. "Let me take your coat, Mr. Weinstock."

"Get out of there for a minute," Mr. Lipman said to Debbie, "and let me see if you are doing a good job."

"I've only done two octaves," Debbie repeated, but she took the wedges out of the strings, picked up the tuning hammer, and slid out.

Mr. Lipman sat down and began to play.

46

"On my piano!" marveled Mrs. Perlman, coming back from hanging up the coats in her hall closet. "Isaac Lipman, playing on my piano!"

Mr. Lipman smiled. "Now, Debbie," he said. "I have traveled all over the world giving concerts, and I have played on pianos tuned by hundreds of different piano tuners—"

"And Grandpa Reuben was the best?" asked Debbie.

"That's right."

"Well, it's very, very hard to get every note dead on, the way he does," she told him.

"It would be almost impossible with that kind of tuning hammer," said Mr. Weinstock. "It's no good. The handle is too long. I'm surprised you didn't break any strings."

"Then I think she did pretty well!" said Mr. Lipman.

"And what tuning fork did you use?" her grandfather asked her. "This? It's all rusted." He hit it against his shoe and held it to his ear. "It doesn't play a true C any more, Debbie."

Debbie's eyes filled with tears.

"Come," said Mr. Lipman, getting up from the piano. "I want to take you all out to lunch."

"My husband will be coming home for lunch soon," said Mrs. Perlman. "I've got a big meal ready, so please stay and eat with us."

"Ah," said Isaac Lipman. "A home-cooked meal . . ."

"It would be a great honor to have you."

"Thank you."

"It is very kind of you, Mrs. Perlman," said Reuben Weinstock, "and I am sorry about your piano. I'll come and tune it first thing tomorrow."

Mrs. Perlman put her arm around Debbie. "Please don't say anything more about it," she said.

"And now," said Isaac Lipman, "I would like to hear Debbie play."

"Play the Mendelssohn *Reverie,* Debbie," said Mr. Weinstock. "We will all remember that the piano is out of tune."

Mrs. Perlman and the two men sat down, and Debbie went to the piano.

"Is there anything you would rather play?" Isaac Lipman asked her when she was done. "Is there any other piece that you like to play better than this one?"

"No," said Debbie.

Mr. Lipman shook his head sadly, smiling at Mr. Weinstock.

"I think she will be a very lovely piano teacher someday," Mrs. Perlman said kindly, getting up to go to the kitchen.

"The world would be a better place if people who did not like to play the piano did not teach the piano," said Mr. Lipman. "Everybody should take the responsibility for finding out what it is he really wants to do."

"I want to be a piano tuner," said Debbie. "And I want to be as good as my grandpa."

"Right now, you had better go home and put

on a dress," Mr. Weinstock told her. "And don't stop to tune any more pianos on the way. Come straight back here, because we must have lunch in plenty of time before the concert."

"Wait until she hears you play!" he said to Isaac Lipman, after he had helped Debbie on with her coat and hat and opened the front door for her. "And if that doesn't inspire her . . ."

"I think it *will* inspire her," chuckled Mr. Lipman. "I think it will inspire her to want to tune grand pianos for concert pianists."

Mr. Weinstock laughed. "If that's the case," he said, "then maybe I had better teach her how."

"Well, I think you should, Reuben. It seems to me she has a real talent for it."

"Yes, I was amazed at how well she was doing!

But, you know, I wanted something better for her."

"What could be better than doing what you love?" asked Mr. Lipman.

At the concert, Debbie and Mr. Weinstock and Mr. and Mrs. Perlman sat in the first row of seats, a little bit over to the left, so they could watch Isaac Lipman's hands.

Everybody in town seemed to have heard that he had come, and all the seats in the Auditorium quickly filled with dressed-up and excited people, who rose to their feet clapping and shouting "Bravo!" when the lights went down and the famous pianist walked out onto the stage.

He bowed to the audience and, sweeping back his long coattails, sat down at the piano. Everyone

in the audience held his breath while Mr. Lipman sat with his head bowed and his hands in his lap. After he had raised them to the keyboard and begun to play the first piece on the program, a long fantasy and fugue by Bach, everyone began to breathe again.

They clapped loudly when it was over, and Mr. Lipman stood beside the grand piano and bowed. Then he swept back his coattails and sat down again, looking at his hands in his lap. The audience waited quietly, and he began to play a sonata in three movements by Beethoven.

At the end of the first movement, Mr. Perlman and Debbie clapped, but Mrs. Perlman and Mr. Weinstock did not. Debbie was amazed. "Didn't you think it was good?" she asked her grandfather.

"It isn't over yet," he said.

After the second movement no one clapped, but after the third, which was really the end of the piece, everyone clapped and shouted "Bravo! Bravo!" Mr. Lipman bowed and left the stage, but the clapping and calling continued until he came back to bow two more times. Then the lights came on and everybody got up to walk around.

"That was good," said Debbie.

"You liked it!"

"Yes. No matter how hard he played, the piano stayed in tune. You did such a good job," said Debbie.

"It sounds as if you've got an assistant there, Mr. Weinstock," said Mr. Perlman.

"Sh-h," whispered Mrs. Perlman. "He doesn't

want her to be a piano tuner! He wants her to be a pianist."

"What's wrong with being a—" began Mr. Perlman, but the lights started to dim and everyone went back to their seats.

On the second half of the program, Isaac Lipman played two rhapsodies by Brahms, and *Carnaval,* by Schumann. At the end of the concert the audience clapped and clapped and called "Encore! Encore!" until he came out on the stage again and sat back down at the piano. He looked out at the audience and said, "A waltz by Chopin."

"Ah-h-h," said the audience.

They clapped and clapped when it was over. Mr. Lipman bowed and left the stage. The audience kept clapping, and he came back, bowed, and left the stage again. The audience kept on clapping until he came back and sat down at the piano again: *Reverie, by Mendelssohn."*

"Oh-h-h," murmured the audience, and Isaac Lipman played the same piece Debbie had played that morning. After he finished, bowed, and left the stage, Mr. Weinstock, still clapping, said to Debbie, "Wouldn't you like to be able to play it like that?"

"No," said Debbie. "Grandpa Reuben—"

Mr. Lipman came back onto the center of the stage, bowed again and again, and went out. Then the lights came on in the Auditorium, and the concert was over.

"Grandpa Reuben, please let me be a piano tuner," said Debbie.

"We must go backstage and say goodbye to Mr. Lipman now," said Mr. Weinstock. "He will be leaving right away."

The whole audience was pushing backstage to shake hands with the great pianist. "Please, Grandpa Reuben," said Debbie. "Please teach me how to be a good piano tuner!"

"What's wrong with being a piano tuner?" asked Mr. Perlman. "Especially a good one!"

"Nothing," said Mr. Weinstock. "Debbie—"

They had come near Mr. Lipman by this time, and even though he was talking to some other people, he reached out and took Debbie by the hand. "You must come to the City and tune my piano sometime," he said.

"Yes, but first I am going to teach her how to

do it," said Mr. Weinstock. "I was just about to say so."

Isaac Lipman was as delighted as Debbie. "So even after hearing one of my concerts, you would rather tune pianos than play them," he said. "Well, I was just like that at your age. I could only think of one thing. For me, of course, it was playing! When I get back to the City, Debbie, I am going to send you a leather bag of your own, filled with good tuning instruments."

"Thank you very much!" said Debbie. "And—"

"Yes?"

"And regulating tools too, Mr. Lipman? Key pliers and bending pliers and a key spacer and parallel pliers and a capstan screw regulator and a capstan wrench and a spring adjusting hook and a spoon bending iron and—"

Some of the people who were standing near them were laughing.

"Everything!" cried Mr. Lipman. "I will ask the head of the piano factory for one of everything."

"Except the tools that I invented," put in Mr. Weinstock. "But I am going to make those for her, and she will be the only other piano tuner to have them."

Debbie put her hand into his. "I'll be just like you," she said.

Now early every morning Debbie Weinstock jumps quickly out of bed and runs downstairs to wash her face and brush her teeth at the kitchen sink. She puts water on to boil in the blue and white enameled saucepan and the old yellow coffee pot, and sets the table with the blue plate and the orange plate, the navy-blue bowl and the green bowl, the plaster salt and pepper shakers with sea-shells stuck into them and bright red plastic tops, the knives and spoons with yellow plastic handles, two white paper napkins, and two big white cups.

Then she goes out into the hall to wake up her grandfather. "Hm-m-m-m-m," she sings in front of his closed bedroom door. "Hm-m-m-m-m."

"Hm-m-m-m-m," comes Mr. Weinstock's voice on the exact same note. "Hm-m-m-m-m. I think we are both right this morning, Debbie."

She takes her shining new tuning fork out of its case, hits it against her knee, and holds it,

singing, to her ear. "We *are* right, Grandpa Reuben!" she says, and goes upstairs to get dressed and make her bed while Mr. Weinstock is getting up.